# THE HOUSE WITH MANY ROOMS

## MICHAEL ROMANO

**The House with Many Rooms**



ISBN: 9798553995430

# THE HOUSE WITH MANY ROOMS

# CHAPTER ONE
## A NEW HOUSE WITH A TWIST ON STRANGE

Hi, my name is Lorenzo. Today, we move into the second house of my whole life of fifteen years, oh and of my sister Olivia's fourteen.

As we pull up with Dad, both our eyes start at the ground floor, scanning up...and up...four stories and a full attic with "dormer" type windows everywhere!

(See top of house on back cover

Those things sticking out of roof)

As Dad stepped out, put his hands on his suspenders and took a deep breath. We could see that he was proud of his purchase.

So, out we jumped, with our best faces said, "Wow Dad, what a great place!"

Dad smiled, nodded and did the triumphant strut to the front door, holding a "Skeleton key" in his hand.

Looking to Lorenzo, Olivia leaned over whispering, "How old can this place be?" He gave me a nervous "I dunno look" and we were in.

Dad looked back saying that this place was made before the turn of the "Last" century. "Yep, somewhere around the 1880's," he proudly said.... "or so," he mumbled.

"The original owner was an assistant to Nicola Tesla. He visited here, even sleeping and holding experiments in this very house.

Don't be surprised if we find some of the neatest things in this place and that," Dad almost giggled to us being so excited. Oh, you see, Dad is an electrical engineer and somewhat of a "Mad Scientist" in his own right.

Olivia and I helped with all the unloading, then went to explore.

"Well, if we were going to live in a haunted castle, let's scare up some ghosts," I said to Olivia. She kind-a half...maybe quarter smiled, then followed me upstairs into who knew what. Little did we know, soon, we'd find out what "WHAT" was!

**END CHAPTER ONE**

# CHAPTER TWO
## OLIVIA...THIS SWITCH, IT'S REALLY WANTING ME TO FLICK IT!

"This place is really weird Olivia," I said.

"But ya know, Renz, some of these things are seriously strange, but kinda interesting.

We looked at each other for a moment, smiled, shook our heads and agreed.

Into the first room on the top floor, there were old pieces of furniture, different wires hanging from poles and most strange were lamps, of a sort, without any plugs at all.

Over in the corner, was a walk-in closet. Lots of old time, stinky suits, some of this and of that, but nothing truly interesting.

Then, dragging my hand across the wall on the way out, I felt a lever. I said, "Olivia, what do you make of this," pointing to it? "Well pull it, why don'tcha," she snapped?!

Reaching up, lifting the thin piece of wood, a panel popped open revealing a room at least five times as large as the large one we were in.

The walls were shiny, even though covered with a hundred years of dust and cobwebs. In the middle of the room, was a chair large enough to fit both my sister and myself, easily.

Against the far wall, behind a steel and glass wall, was an amazing panel of bizarre knobs, dials and some of the old time tubes grandpa had in that ancient TV he claimed to watch.

Then there was a large throw switch, kind of like the one in that horror flick we watched a few months ago.

"I don't think we should mess with anything at this time," Olivia said as I nodded "Yes."

Out in the hallway, each few feet seemed to give us things to wonder about, but when we walked into the next room, we had to just stand and stare.

"Yeah, Renzo...what the heck do you make of that," Olivia said, pointing to the gigantic maps and pictures of times and places on every wall!


**END CHAPTER TWO**

# CHAPTER THREE
## WE'D BETTER READ UP
## ON THIS TESLA GUY

Dad called out to us for lunch, and we slid down the banisters, reaching the kitchen before him.

Looking for lunch, we noticed some appliances completely different to anything we've ever had or even seen in those "Buy Me" commercials.

In came Dad with a yummy smelling bag of what turned out to be hot Italian sandwiches.

"Dad, what are some of these weird things on the counter," I asked

"Not sure yet, but perhaps we can find out together," he said with a smile. We nodded as the sandwiches were being stuffed into our mouths.

Dad said, "After lunch, you both need to wander around," as if we hadn't already started, "and pick out a bedroom for you two." With a smile and a nod, we were off like a shot.

"Okay Olivia, we maybe should get rooms next to each other so if there are any night adventures in room searching, we stand less of a chance of being caught." Olivia put two fingers to her nose signifying yes, oh...one finger to her nose showed "no" or "Danger."

After ten rooms and an hour later, I heard a yell from way upstairs. Climbing higher and higher, I came to the stairs to the attic. Into it I went and there was Olivia standing in the middle of a "Mad Scientists'" laboratory.

We looked at each other saying, "Oh, this must be "IT," at the same time!

To the left wall, which was to the back yard, was a bank of ten foot tall stained glass windows that glowed with the afternoon sun. All around the huge room were so many gadgets and gizmos our head spun, twirling around and pointing at them.

"Let's start cleaning up all the dust and little bug critters so we may bring up our stuff," I said.

By four o'clock it was pretty spit shiny, ready to move in. So, we commenced to check out the walls for secret stuff and into the trunks we did go.

They all were locked, but with such an antique locking system, they were no match for my Camp-king Boy Scout pocket knife and Olivia's bobby pins.

The first sprung open with a "B'doing!" As we slowly opened the squeaky top it was obvious that it contained..."MONEY!"

After a moment, we noticed that it wasn't regular money, but that it was from many countries, and even, "Times!"

Olivia scratched her head saying, "Travelers?" I added, "Just what kind?"

Searching through, we found monies from Ancient Greece, all the way to the forties, from almost every country on earth.

Then, just as I was about to close the lid, for now, Olivia pulled up a pouch of coins jingling. Opening them, the coins had a shape similar to a small pyramid containing a glowing set of numbers on each, that jingled like church bells when shaken. Well we thought they were numbers, but not in any language or alphabet we knew.

"What country," I started to ask?

"Or what world," Olivia kicked in," half nervously laughing.

"This would need much further investigation, and I think we've pretty well burned up enough brains and theories for the first day, don't you think?"

She looked at the money, then me, nodded, saying..."Hey, maybe the yard will be less stressing."

I agreed and down and out we went.

Well, you guessed it...we were some kind-a way wrong!

## END CHAPTER THREE

MICHAEL ROMANO    17

# MY ODD CHAPTER
## THE YARD, AND .... "WILL YA LOOK AT THAT!"

Out back, first thing seen was this great wall of a hedge, twelve feet tall & thick that seemed to go far in all directions.

"Look, Renz, over there," Olivia pointed way right, "a slit in the thicket."

Well, can't stop just for a little strange feeling in the stomach, so, through it we went.

Weaving as if in a maze, we came out what seemed to be fifty paces later into what I could only say was this field of statues, globes, and seriously weird, well, can't even imagine what most of them were.

"Lorenzo...look at this world statue." It has little holes drilled into it all over."

On its base was a smaller throw switch, similar to the behemoth one upstairs. This one I was gonna throw!

"Here goes," I said to my sisters loud "No!!" Too late.

With a hummmmm, and creak, followed by crunching, the globe slowly turned as the holes began to glow, dust along with little chunks of I could not begin to think what, popped off of it.

"Hey, cool," I said to my sister's stunned look, pointing as if she had built the dang thing herself.

Points of light that seemed only to reach a few inches beyond the large stone globe and no farther.

"Look," Olivia said curiously... "Some of the lit spots match up to the money we found upstairs." Only a very few seemed to shoot up into the sky...hmmm.

Too much to see and not laboring on the strange money, we wandered all over.

Many alcoves, nooks & crannies that were cut in the hedges were now grown over, but we pulled back branches to marvel at wonderous mix mash of craft, sculptures, machines and things we had no idea what were...Heck we didn't know what "Any" of them were!

"Hey, over there," Olivia pointed and started running towards a tall vine encrusted object.

Taking the twenty minutes it took pulling down eighty year old vines to open it up to the light of day again. There it stood.

Looking each other we both said... "There "What" stood?!

Eight tall, near ten foot, carved pillars. "It feels like marble," I said...with a dome atop, eight feet deep stairs all around, stepped up to the platform within.

All kindsa carvings on the floor, each within a pie shaped space of its own.

"Yeah, we gotta find out what "This" is Olivia!"

"Wait, ...look at that space." "There is a carving and symbols on that triangle coin we found up in that room, hmmm."

"You don't think," she asked?

"Just...maybe we are standing on a platform to other places," I said even amazing myself.

"Or times," Olivia barely whispered.

"Right now, we have to get back to the house, find a room and get situated...we have some serious adventures ahead and I don't want to miss one, you, Olivia?"

"But we have to get back to this," she said with an excited giggle.

A nod and a look towards the house, she gave start to "The race was on.

She was a girl...but the fastest one I'd ever met!

## END OF MY ODD CHAPTER

# CHAPTER FOUR
# NOW WHERE DOES THIS TUNNEL LEAD?

Setting up our room was easier than we thought. Wide halls and doors gave to easy room entry for beds and things. Dad and a helper brought them upstairs, while Olivia and I wrestled them in the room. Having the beds set up, we went down for dinner and decided to finish the rest in the morning.

Dad called out saying he'd made a great meal for us. I looked at sis with a curious stare saying, "He cooked?"

As we slid the last banister to the main floor, we could smell what he'd cooked. Pizza!

Well, this was supremely Okay with us, as we all plopped around the monster table in the dining room for some slices of

Mushroom and Sausage pizza with a big cold glass of milk direct from Dad's cooler.

Being tired hit us pretty fast, after the late dinner, so Olivia and I went upstairs, a bit more slowly this time,

I dropped onto my bed, while sis sat down thinking, she wasn't as tired.

We spoke for a few minutes, then she leaned over and was "Out."

Thoughts of what may be all over this house filled my dreams, and I swore I could hear people trying to speak to me in those dreams...hmmm.

Tomorrow will bring many surprises. Some wonderful and a few just downright different. Ohhhhh welllll.

The morning sun hit the grand stained glass windows and bathed us both in an amazing rainbow of wakening. It was the start of a most remarkable day of enlightenment. (Understanding many new things)

Dad wasn't up as I looked at my watch seeing it wasn't yet 6 o'clock.

"Heck Olivia, we beat the rooster up!" This got a short laugh, cause she wasn't completely up either.

"A room to room search was in order, plus she needed to bring her journal in which she keeps, to take notes.

With great curiosity, we wrote as much on each room, sketches included, so as to have some direction in which to proceed.

Not a room was empty on the third floor, just beneath the attic, and all things found were to do with things not always similar to each other.

Some rooms had a multitude (whole bunch) of electrical wonders. Another had very large spinning mirrors with what seemed beams from some large strange shaped bulbs.

Each one with a more confusing thing than the last. "Renzo, it'll take us years to figure all these things out," she said.

"Well, good thing we're young!" Olivia gave out with a belly laugh, and I followed. (deep down loud laugh)

Holding my hand out to her bowing, I said, "Well Ma'am, shall we proceed?"

With a grin she said, "Nothing I'd rather do." Off we went skipping down the hall to the next curious encounter.

## END CHAPTER FOUR

# CHAPTER FIVE
## MY MIND WENT BACK TO THE SPINNING MIRRORS ROOM

"Olivia, we need to go back to that spinning mirrors room, cause I can swear I heard voices in it!"

"What...Me too!" "I just didn't say anything, as not to have you think I was crazy. Let's go!"

Back down the long eight foot wide hallway we ran, till we stood in front of the door. Both of us could feel a presence there. So thick, you could grab it! Into it we slowly walked. Ever moving our heads from side to side waiting for a face to jump out of somewhere...we weren't sure what to expect.

Searching the room for clues, we came across a pile of books in the corner nestled in a wooden box, by date, it seemed.

We each took a pile and plowed through the words, sketches and didn't know what the heck these squiggly lines meant.

"Renzo, Renzo... Here is a short diagram and explanation of what it does, oh, and on the second page, how to use it, I think."

Reading on, Olivia said,

"The spinning mirrors, produce a light, when acted on by these blue bulbs, and allow us to see events that have already happened. Let's see, that's in reverse, counter clockwise. What would happen in clockwise, I wonder?"

"Let us not get ahead of ourselves," I said. "Here, everything needs to be cleaned, and the wires checked as not to blow up!"

A cleaning we went for the better part of an hour and a half of polishing and checking till Olivia said, "I do believe we are ready brother."

"I do believe you are correct," as we both laughed a bit too similar to a mad scientist for my taste.

Flicking, Lord knows "How" many switches, the book said to slowly turn the largest dial to the left.

"Throw the large switch to get all the 'big' electricity going," I said to Olivia.

The crackle of electricity popped all over the room, from tall poles to equipment, scaring the heck out of us.

A "hummmm" progresses into a growl as the angled mirrors began to sway, spin and sparkle.

The faster the spin, the way more sparkle, until the room was aglow with seemingly living light!

In the center we could see the vague figures of a ship...a pirate ship.

Men in that type clothes were on a ship huddled to one side, for what we didn't know.

Then all of a sudden, we could hear them. Screaming orders to fire a broadside, seeing the cannons blasting at a nearby ship.

The pirates pulled up against the other ship and swung over with their cutlasses waving and pistols firing.

I quickly ran to the wall of switches and shut them off, then sat down.

Olivia was completely freaked and sat beside me. "How the heck did you do that," she questioned, "and why is my shirt wet with sea water?"

"Not a clue, but before we try 'THAT' again, we surely need to read a whole lot more."

She leaned back on the floor and all she said was "Yes sir!"


**END CHAPTER FIVE**

# CHAPTER SIX
# BACK TO THE ROOM
# WITH THE TUNNEL

Back to looking around the Mirrors room and that "tunnel like" door in the very far wall.

The door itself seemed to be made of serious four inches by one foot boards, with old time square finger sized nails in it. Six feet across, it also had metal straps if that were six inches wide by what had to be half an inch thick seemingly there to keep someone from coming through to this side not us out.

There was a bronze clapper like door puller to open it. That is if anyone could figure how to spring the lock.

Reading through the rest of the morning, Olivia found several pages pertaining (about) the "fort door," as we called it. "Here, here's a diagram of the construction," Olivia shouted from across the room.

"Let's see, there is a long, trench link cut in the floor covered by another wooden plank, over to, ah, ah...There," she said!

Following it to the end was a small box on the wall. Opening it, showed us a smaller throw switch like in the movies. "Well," she said, "go ahead."

Slowly touching the switch with my fingers, down I pulled and there I heard a "Klunk!"

A small six inch by six inch door sprung open in the front.

Trying to see in the dark hole proved impossible, but Olivia shouted "Stop!"

"There was a page, lemme see." Through the book she went page by page till, "I have it. 7...10... 56, is the code."

Well, now comes the time. Reaching my hand in, oh yes, slowly, my fingers feel buttons. Which way is "One?"

"Go ahead," Olivia said.

"Yeah, go ahead," I mumbled to my self. 7 10 56 I think I pressed and "Sproing!" the door unlocked and sprung loose ever so little. Just enough for us to get a finger hold to pull it open.

Now that it was open, what kind-a freaky thing lay on the other side?

Gathering up a lot of nerve, we both gave it a pull and it swung open as easy as you please.

"Well, will you look at that," said Olivia!


## END CHAPTER SIX
## GOTTA LOOK NOW!

# CHAPTER SEVEN
## WE NEVER WERE REALLY ALONE
## & OKAY ... WHO IS THAT?

As the door swung open, a cloud with flickering beams of lights shot here and there. Almost like a laser light show.

Then, after several moments, they got more, or...well, together and something started to form.

The silhouette (outline) of a man started to appear. He waved to us, as not to appear frightening. Such a smile wouldn't scare anyone.

"Hello, my children, my name is Nicola, and yours?"

I looked beck at Olivia saying, "This is only a hologram."

"Then how does it know we are kids?"

I shrugged my shoulders then said, "I am Lorenzo, and this is my sister Olivia."

"Very pleased to meet you, to be truthful, I'm very pleased to meet anyone," as he laughed a bit then smiled. "How did you come to be here this day...it is day isn't it?"

"Well, ah, yes. Our Dad bought this house and all the doodads (things and oddities) in it."

"Well, that could be wonderful, if you allow me to teach you how they all work," Nicola said.

With smiles to our ears, we gleefully shook our heads yes and he then started to teach as we took the cross legged squat position.

We asked if he would start with the spinning mirrors. He told us that they were a bit dangerous, but he thought we could be careful enough and he started in with what they had the possibility for.

"The mirrors have the capability to, not only show scenes from the past, but sounds and even, by some odd side effect, smells."

"Turning the master dial to the left allows one to go into the past, stopping at times and places long gone by."

Raising my hand, as if in school, he waived it down saying, "Just ask." What happens if we turn the master dial to the right?"

Tilting his head down, said, "We only did it once and saw more than we wished we ever had, so it was a pact we had never to do it again."

"Read the book numbered '24' where the instructions are laid out very simply. There are possibilities which we never tried as there was so much work and only the few of us...but who knows?"

I said, "I do believe, Olivia, he meant traveling into the past in our solid form, what do you think?"

"I think we have a 'Lot' of reading to do before anything like that," Olivia said, sounding like Dad.

"Yeah, I think so too."

Then...he then faded away, back into the void. (Emptiness)

**END CHAPTER SEVEN**
**YEP... A WHOLE, "NEW"**
**KINDA FREAKY!**

   THE HOUSE WITH MANY ROOMS

# CHAPTER EIGHT
## LET'S KEEP DAD OUT OF THE LOOP FOR NOW

Dad's contracting business was doing so well, that he and Olivia and I were able to take the summer off. His field supervisors, who called in daily several times, completed the jobs Dad had started at the beginning of summer. Dad needed that time to renovate a house that hadn't been lived in for half a hundred years or so!

Thank goodness there weren't strange and wonderful things on the ground floor rooms as there were strewn all the heck over the top ones.

Seemed like the ground floor was the living and visiting one...the second, the sleeping and office space. Then there was the third, fourth and the attic. All seemed chock full of strange oddities that we were bound and determined to become familiar with! But, back to the mirrors, and what we needed to do.

#1 Make sure surfaces are clean
#2 Don't lean into the visual area
#3 Keep quiet as they may hear you
#4 Learn emergency shut down
#5 Be aware of time and place to write in ledger of dial spot to year

"Seems easy enough," I said to Olivia. "Let's go and see where it takes us." With a smile and a nod, we were off

Re-wiping the mirrors to a shine, we went over to the dials. As we were told, we marked down in the book the starting numbers, and to where we moved them to. Three large lines and eighteen smaller ones in between were done.

There was the low hum, then more and more, till the sparkles started again. Then the flash in the center expanded into a ten foot wide live movie!

Olivia shushed me as I was "Oh Wowing" a bit too loudly.

Some people in pilgrim clothes were yanking this young lady off to a pile of sticks with a pole in the middle. She was crying, "I'm innocent," but they still yelled names at her.

"Olivia. One of the names was "WITCH!"

"I don't care," she said. "WE need to do something NOW!"

Into the center she stepped and right into their time. Shouting to let her go, waving her hands like a super crazy woman, they did.

She then grabbed the girl by the arm and yanked her into our room, into "Our" time!

I ran to the panel, turned it right the heck off, then turned to introduce ourselves.

"Hello, my name is Lorenzo, and this is my sister Olivia."

She looked, pretty afraid asking, "Are you a witch too?"

This was quickly unsettling, and we asked her if she were a good witch, like in the Wizard of oz, not having much witchery to go on.

"Mostly," she said. Well, that mostly made us feel better.

We just sat in a circle looking at each other till she said, "My name's Elsbeth and I am forever in your debt, how may I serve you Lorenzo and Olivia?"

Now, sis, just one of your ordinary days in Casa Romano!


**END CHAPTER EIGHT
NOT TOO MUCH, WAAAYYY
OUT OF THE ORDINARY**

# CHAPTER NINE
## NOW, WITH A MAGICAL HOUSE, AND A WITCH IN TOW, IT'S OFF TO WORK WE GO

"Excuse me, Lorenzo, but I am so hungry as not to have been fed these three days. Perchance (maybe) you could spare me a crust of bread, please," Elsbeth pleaded.

I looked at Olivia and said, "She's gonna need a crash course in the twenty first century right now, you run down for some milk and cookies and I'll start on her." Olivia nodded yes and off she ran.

"My sister is getting you food, but till she comes back I have several things to tell you about."

"Are you a Wizard"" she asked.

"Of a sort, yes," I answered, only to give some reason for what happened.

"We are from the future, do you understand, "Future?"

She looked at me asking, "You think me an idiot? Of course, I know what the future is," she said a bit grumpily.

"Well, hold on for this," I said. "You are about four hundred years into tomorrow and here in another land safe with us."

Amazingly enough, she took this with great calm, sitting back in the chair I had gotten for her.

"It is a good thing, then, that I am here, safe and with friends." At which point Olivia came in with cookies and milk.

"What is this," Elsbeth asked?

Olivia told her they were her Mom's best cookies and had to go with a cold glass of milk.

With a bite, she took to them like a duck to water, eating mine and Olivia's portions too! But if it made her happy and full, it was all good.

"Exactly what year is it," she asked?

I looked at sis and said..."2016, at the beginning of summer."

Without a word or twitch about it, she asked, "Would it be bad manners if I was to have a few more of your Mom's cookies?"

We smiled and asked her to come down stairs with us to get more.

All the way down, we spoke of new inventions such as cars, televisions, planes, and the such so when she encountered them, they wouldn't frighten her.

In the kitchen, Dad had just put a turkey in the oven on his lunch break when he emerged from the basement but had gone back to since.

"Your kitchen smells 'Magical' Elsbeth said, or really, drooled.

"When it's done, you shall join us for dinner," Olivia said. Elsbeth shook her head yes about six times.

"We must find a room upstairs for you, and an explanation why you need to stay here, to our Father.

Up the stairs we went, Elsbeth with a fist full of cookies in one hand, and another glass of milk in the other saying, "I'm going to like being in 2016!"

**END CHAPTER NINE**

# CHAPTER TEN
## NEED TO BRING ELSBETH
## INTO OUR CIRCLE

Asking Dad if we could eat dinner in our rooms this evening, so as to finish up, he said he'd call when it was time to come on down to pick up the fixins' (All the dinner eats)

Sitting down with Elsbeth, we explained all things about the house, then went directly into the four hundred years she missed. Well, that was a stretch, but she soaked up information like a sponge, every so often asking, "In the air?'" or "Under the sea?" There were so many questions, but between us, our computer and two platefuls of Chocolate chip cookies plus a half gallon of milk, we were just fine.

Heck, by the time we were done, she was almost sounding like us!

As I went down to pick up dinner and all the goodies that go with roast turkey, Elsbeth went and sat in a corner for a moment looking a bit down in spirits.

"What's wrong," Olivia asked?

"My friends are long gone and the family I had is dust now," was her answer.

As I came in with such yummy smelling plates of eats, Elsbeth looked up as I said, "We're your new family now." I smiled large and nodded "Sure!" She smiled, then the smell of a full scale turkey feast hit her and took over.

Like ravenous (Animal hungry) beasts we ate everything and licked clean our plates.

Elsbeth said, she'd never eaten like that in her life and couldn't fit another bite. I turned behind him, pulling out "Three" pieces of whipped cream slathered (Way covered) pumpkin pie for dessert. "Then, should I throw these away," he asked?

She popped up from her Turkey Coma and was on the pie so fast.

"Here young lady, it's easier with a fork," I said. Which she quickly implemented without losing a bite.

Olivia grinned as Elsbeth ate, really well, for the first time in her life.

Now, every nook and cranny of her tiny stomach was full to splitting, I gave her my bed to use and Olivia and I made a temporary one on the floor for me.

Fast asleep, Elsbeth had a glowing smile as I looked at my sister saying, "Well, it's been a fairly full day, don't you think?"

She shook her head, saying goodnight as we both drifted off till tomorrow...and what a tomorrow to come.

**END CHAPTER TEN
AN EASY BREATHER**

# CHAPTER ELEVEN
## NEXT TIME, WE READ FIRST

Taking a break from the, oh so tempting Mirrors room, we went down the hall to the room with the steel door.

It opened with an unexpected "Whooooosh." The air sucked in like a vacuum and, for a second, found it hard to breathe. When the door was unsealed, it was like a clean room with everything polished perfect. No dust, dirt or cobwebs.

Wall to wall, there were tall stainless steel poles with twirly looking tops and all connected to each other, on the floor. Then all the cables came into one, a few feet before their attaching to the big panel in this small room built into the rear wall.

Again, there was a plentiful book library on the wall, but two were on the end. One said, "Instructions in Function," (how it worked)

...the other in "Capabilities" (What it could do).

Knowing better than "Not " to read, we did the yoga sit on the floor and read as Elsbeth looked around.

"Elsbeth, be sure you don't touch anything," I said as she shook her head while being amazed at the contraptions.

Olivia said..."This room has some serious looking electrical equipment in here Renzo. What have you read so far?"

"It says, it is able to transmit live pictures across this long room, and with some 'Tweaking,' as Nicola called it, can go much farther even across a country!"

"Well we'll just see about that," I mumbled to myself.

"Olivia, stand here. Now don't move." Throwing the switch, the arcs of electricity began shooting everywhere, where Elsbeth shot under a desk, and then it settled down.

Much to Olivia's bravery, she didn't move a hair.

Then across the room, a cloud of white and silver began to form on the second platform.

"Look," Olivia shouted, pointing at what was materializing (becoming visible). It, it's "Me," she squealed!

"Move your arm up and down sis. Now turn around, while staying on the platform," I asked.

"Look," Elsbeth said pretty well shocked by now, "There are 'Two' of you."

She was right, a hologram of her, with motion was transmitted (Sent) to another location. What a telephone!!

Wait, there is a microphone in Olivia's station and a switch on the panel saying sound. Maybe..."Click!"

"Say something quietly and I'll run down there to see if I can hear you."

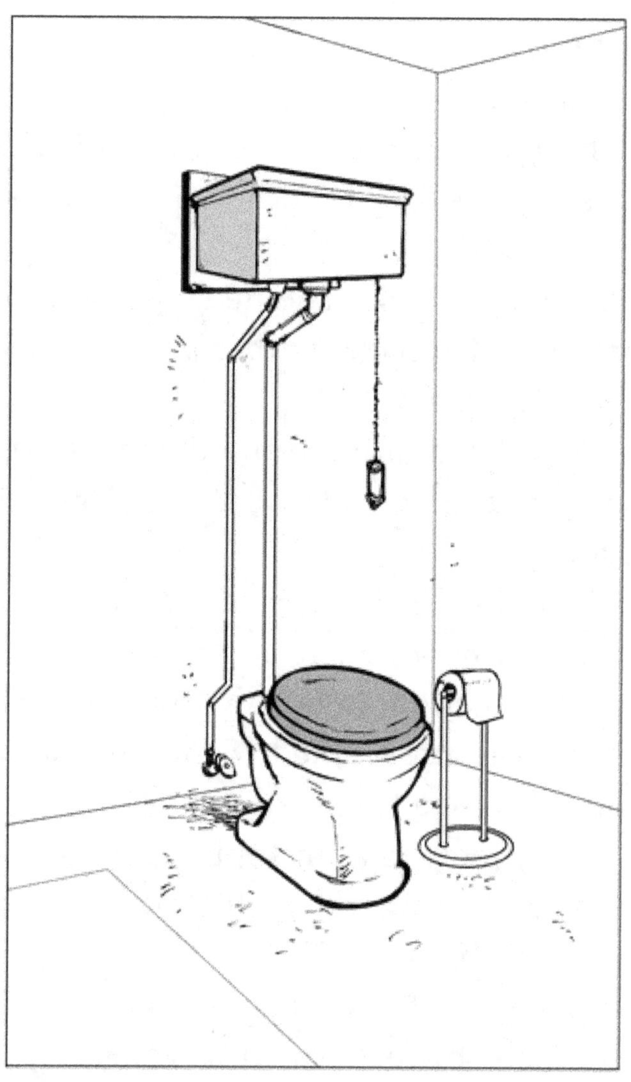

Clear as can be, her voice came through.

I ran back to shut off the controls, saying to Elsbeth that it was Okay to come out. She didn't understand "Okay" but the hand wave did it.

"Wow, what an amazing invention this would have been...what am I saying. Now it will be a killer phone," I said to Olivia.

Elsbeth, quietly whispered in my ear, "Is there a privvy near?"

"A what?"

"Bathing facility with a chamber pot," she said, with me still not getting it.

Then sis said, "Oh, a toilet," and took her by the hand.

With a little, well more than a little explanation, she used the facilities and was properly amazed at indoor plumbing.

Let's see what wonders lay ahead.

"Ok sis, don't forget those two books and put the room number on them so as not to get mixed up."

"Onward and upward," Olivia said with a raised hand!

## END CHAPTER ELEVEN
## BACK TO THE ROUND DOOR

# CHAPTER TWELVE
## STILL ...WHO IS THE MAN BEHIND THE ROUND DOOR?

Explaining all we can as we go along, to Elsbeth, to catch her up those short four hundred years, it may seem as if we tag team talk to her.

We both stopped as we entered the "Round Door" room, to explain to her what we were about to see as not to throw her into freak-out overdrive.

She seemed to take it way better than I would and called it a type of "Spectre" which is half a ghost in wispy form. "So," I said to Olivia, "What the heck, she'll learn this one as we go along!!"

Throwing the switches, unlocking the doors and stepping back, the fog inside began to condense into a form, then a pretty clear person.

"You have returned and with a friend," Nicola said.

"There are so many things I have to tell you about the wonders in this house. Nothing has been removed has it," he asked?

"No," I said. "Our Dad purchased it from a bank who was watching over it, and completely intact. He has no idea what lies above the second floor," I told him.

"What does that mean," he asked?

"There were no inventions below the third floor," I told Nicola.

"That is so far from correct, I could not explain, but need to show you," he responded.

"How, are you confined by walls of the door?"

Nicola said, "There are five doors in the house, here is a map to them and scattered machines," as he handed it to me a good sized spark snapped my back on my rump!

"Sorry, I forgot about the transfer power from one dimension to another," he said.

"One what to another where? Oh, we'll get to that later, let me look at this."

Let's find Dad and make sure he doesn't end up in some other time, ship himself to the moon, or something worse," Olivia said.

We took Elsbeth with us, who by now was getting used to many odd things, as regular events. What a great girl.

Down the banisters we slid as Elsbeth ran next to us down the stairs. Gotta show her how to slide.

We could hear Dad hammering in the basement and went straight there.

Olivia whispered, "How do you plan to tell Dad my genius brother?"

"Yeah, well... I'm not quite sure this is the right time, but we have to keep Dad away from harm.

Forgetting, for a moment of our visitor of time past, we came up to Dad as he looked sort of sideways at Elsbeth.

"And who may this lovely lady be, all dressed up in...well, whatever, it is interesting," he said

"Dad, let's sit down for lunch and we'll tell you a great story," I said slowly.

"Sounds great, let's all go out for a mid-day Pizza, Okay," Dad said with a big grin.

Into the car we all went. Had to pull Elsbeth in at first, with a bit of fighting.

As we started to drive, she grabbed hold of the seats and clammed up.

"Dad, this house is more than you think ..."Waaaay more."

Telling him who it belonged to, he said he knew the name, but not exactly who Tesla was.

A quick and in depth discussion of his feats and inventions amazed Dad pretty darn much.

"And what has this got to do with the house?" he asked.

"Mostly above the second floor, his inventions are all still here. Olivia and I have been reading his notes."

"Well, son and daughter, what do they do?" Dad asked.

"Things we better explain on a full stomach," I said. He nodded approval but did ask if one of the contraptions gave us the little witch girl?

Sis and I nodded our head, Elsbeth was still grasping to the seats for dear life but shook her head.

Dad said, "Okay then, what are we having for lunch?"

"That went way better than I thought," I whispered to Olivia. She gave a deep breath of relief as did Elsbeth when we parked.

**END CHAPTER TWELVE
THIS CAN'T BE.**

# CHAPTER THIRTEEN
# DON'T KNOW WHAT THIS PIZZA IS ...BUT I LIKE IT

Elsbeth got brave when the odor of fresh baked "Pizza" slid up her nose. "Is THAT" what we're having as she touched her nose?

Dad smiled and nodded as we sat her down at a table.

Mr. Romano delivered two specials of mushroom, sausage and pepperoni.

Elsbeth watched as I picked the thin crust delicacy up in two hands and shoved the end in my mouth.

She did too, and a squeal of ecstasy came from her mid chew.

"Well," Olivia said, "she's one of us now!"

We drove by the park to let Elsbeth out with me, as Olivia always spoke with Dad better, and she started in with a smile and a little facial twitch.

After forty five minutes, and six or seven wave offs of the duo out in the playground, I was done.

Dad just sat there. Staring off a bit into space, he finally spoke.

"Can I find a deal or what?!"

I was so shocked at "That" response, I started to laugh. He did too and asked, "Do you, as the 'A' students in a school for advanced achievers, have a hold on all this?"

"Well, Dad, yes, we do," I answered.

"Then," he said, "When you need my help, call me, otherwise we can have an evening up to date at dinner."

I could only shake my head, "Yes," And waved the wild bunch back into the car.

Home we drove, by the Ice Cream shop, at Elsbeth's request. Dad asked me quietly, "Does she always eat like this?"

"So far, yes," I whispered.

At home, Dad went back to work as the three of us burped in unison (Together at same time) and went back to the round door room.

Pulling the lever and popping it open, then turning the power dial we read off in the, well...operating manual...the image came in clearer.

There he was, sharper, more able to see us, as we him.

"Hello, my little friends, and who is the smaller lady?" Nicola said.

"Oh, she's Elsbeth. She's sort of from the seventeenth century," I said. Renzo winced and Elsbeth smiled as she was still on a Pizza/Ice Cream high.

The apparition, who was Nicola, became clearer for a moment as he blew his top. "You went inside the Spinning Mirrors, didn't you?!"

"Well, Olivia saw the towns people ready to burn Elsbeth, jumped in and saved her," I said in our defense.

At that moment, Elsbeth, having watched us with some of the dials, decided on her own to spin "His" dial to make him clearer.

Giving it a "Carnival" guess the number on the wheel spin, there occurred an explosion in the doorway!

Nicola disappeared.

We heard a moan from across the room...There was Nicola, "Whole!" No vapor, not a ghost, but completely all there.

He stood up, touching himself, arms, legs, body and finally head.

"I'm alive!!! All here and alive," he screamed!!

Dad must have heard him scream, as he was in the doorway in nothing flat.

Seeing the smoke in the doorway, and the "I'm sorry look on her face," our ancient friend Elsbeth had, Dad figured some of it out.

Then he saw the old time clothes on the guy in front of him.

"Is he...?"

"Oh yeah, Dad," Renzo said.

"Another mouth to feed, son." "Stop now, or I'll have to get another job to feed them," Dad smiled and said.

I looked at him and he took my hand saying, "I know you are probably more able to deal with this than I, but remember, I'm here for any reason."

Olivia ran up and hugged him as I gave him the two fingered salute to which he responded on the way out the door.

Olivia said to me, "Darn, we have a great Dad!"

Dad, turning to the previously exploded ghost asked, "And 'who' are you?"

Holding out his hand, saying, "I am Nicola, pleased to meet you more than you could ever know."

Olivia and I were mute (Not talking) just standing there, looking at him then at each other, and back to him.

Seeming to take it in stride, or other things on his mind gave him to just take it as normal for us, went back to the house business.

Nicola seemed to be busy for a moment looking at both sides of his hands and we were just trying to remember how to breathe.

Give us a moment and we'll get back to you.


## END CHAPTER THIRTEEN
## IT'S NEAR TIME

# CHAPTER FOURTEEN

"So, "You" Know How to Work These Machines," Olivia asked.

"Seems You Young Ones Found Some New Twists," said Tesla!

"Are you the 'Real' Tesla, Nicola Tesla?" Olivia beat getting it out of our mouths!

"I do believe I am," he said, feeling up and down the solidness of his arms.

"Don't know what you did, but it was way past any experiment I ever did," he said.

This is amazing, I said to myself.

"We read that you died in early "1943," I said.

"January 7th to be exact. Only I didn't exactly die."

"What's didn't exactly mean... exactly," Olivia asked?

"My assistant, under my guidance, transferred my being, into a pure form of electricity that was able to maintain itself within the confines of the round room sheathed (all covered inside) with silver.

When I appeared to have died, I could no longer speak with any one from the outside world, until the door was again opened by you two...and blown up by her (pointing at Elsbeth) to make me what I now am!"

"This is so amazing. I hadn't a single clue that this could ever be possible," he kept saying.

Looking at Elsbeth, Nicola asked, "Just what did you do? Please show me."

Walking back to the dials, she grabbed..."No, Don't," yelled Tesla! "Please don't touch as it may send me back. Just point," he asked of her.

Pointing at the largest dial, she made a big sweeping movement as if she spun the dial all the way around.

"Aha, much more clarity and power, over powered the connections and caused a loop that exploded inwards."

"Hold on sir, your way past our training, and no need to go on as long as 'You' know what happened," I said.

He nodded as did we but explained we had made farther strides than did he with some of his other creations.

"Please allow me to see your electricity fuse box," he asked.

We went down stairs then outside to the connection box.

"What are these switches, where are the large fuses?" Nicola said.

"Several years ago, all the electrical was changed to 'Circuit Breakers'...and the larger homes, which this one surely stacks up to be, was given much more power to

I threw the switch and the mirrors began to spin. Odd, but not as fast, noticed by Tesla. When Olivia said, "That's when I threw the second switch."

We both in unison asked, "What other switch?"

"This one on the wall marked supplemental (Extra juice).

I could barely hear Nicola say to himself..."And a child shall lead them."

"Oh, by the way, Mr. Tesla, I am Lorenzo Maximilian, this is my sister Olivia Eleanor and this is Elsbeth...ahhh, just Elsbeth for now.

"You have no idea of how glad I am to meet you, meet anybody," Tesla answered!

**END THE LONG CHAPTER FOURTEEN**

# CHAPTER FIFTEEN
## WITH SUCH LITTLE INFORMATION, WE CAN NOW JUMP AHEAD SO FAR

We are all in the "Hall of Mirrors," as Nicola calls it, showing the steps we took to open the portal into the past, so clearly.

Polishing the mirrors, as we took the book's instructions as law, Tesla smiled at our preparations.

Setting the dials as before, we looked to him as he gestured with his hand to go ahead. "This is your experiment," he said, "Do what you will!"

Making sure the mirrors were locked down in just the same direction, Olivia gave me the sign, "All is fine."

As she, Elsbeth and Nicola stepped back, I threw the switch, setting the gauges to the past, as before, then slowly turned the power dial.

Spinning mirrors and the growing ball of light, in the middle, became a show of the past clear as a bell.

"Look," Nicola said with a raised voice. "It's so much clearer than my time!"

There were the puritans, men all dressed up in knee pants, shirts with large collars and large buckle shoes, the women with their long dark dresses, lace collars and those white nurse hats all starched atop their heads.

"So peaceful a group who only a while ago were ready to burn Elsbeth," Olivia said, with a bit of anger in her voice.

"Remember, my colleagues, people aren't always as they seem, so pick your friends so carefully. People are the same then, now and a thousand years either in the past or future. When you find a friend, be good and honest with them."

"I feel that you three are my friends," as he smiled, then we looked back at what was happening amid the mirrors.

"How about we turn back the hands of time and see what we may see," Nicola asked.

All of us were in accordance (Said yes) so, he said, "Back up a few centuries."

"Fine by me," as I picked Northern Europe (Didn't know I could direct the place till Nicola pointed to the year dial) about the tenth century.

"Look," Olivia said, "Vikings in their long dragon headed ships!"

"How close can we get without being noticed," I asked?

At that moment a rather large Viking stood tall and bellowed, holding his sword high, "Hvem er det."

Quickly pulling out my cell phone and typing in what I believed him to say, came back the translation of,

"Who goes there?"

At that very same moment, Nicola said," about that close!"

"Somehow," Nicola said, "with the enriched power supply, cross viewing can be possible. Hmmm, I will have to study that," he mumbled.

Olivia was almost face to face with a six and a half foot quite armed perturbed (Dad's word for grumpy and unhappy with what's going on) man from a group of people who didn't do much smiling unless they were fighting an enemy. Which we may very well be perceived (thought I was) of at this very moment.

Using the program on my phone, Olivia typed in, "How are you today, I am a visitor," pressed the button and out came the words at they should be.

Now this gave the giant warrior such a shock to hear a small little thing in my hand speak to him, he smiled and gestured to me to see it.

"Well what do you know, she can make friends anywhere," said Nicola. I smiled in agreement and told her to speak with him for a minute, through the translator, then say goodbye and back the heck up into the portal.

She shook her head a bit nervously, as the Viking could only see and hear her. Olivia held out her hand, gently grasped his, said, " Ha det," which is good bye, backed up, then the flash closing the doorway quickly as she came home.

"What a workout for my nerves that was," she said while breathing pretty hard.

"I do think we shall have many more heavy breathing moments," said Nicola.

Even Elsbeth agreed with that!

**END CHAPTER FIFTEEN**

# CHAPTER SIXTEEN
## "HOW WOULD YOU LIKE TO CONTROL LIGHTNING," NICOLA ASKED?

Well, we didn't need to take long answering that question so, with a jump in his step, we followed Nicola to the side wall of the attic.

"Where now," Elsbeth asked, touching the wall all over.

He reached up high, pulling on this thin chain that hung almost invisibly against the wall.

A portion of the wall backed in, then slid to the left, leaving a six foot wide opening.

Inside, unknown to us as the attic was so large, was another good sized room, with these tall thick poles, topped by globes the size of a beach ball.

"Let's clean up a bit, wouldn't want a massive 'Dust' explosion now, would we," Nicola said with a smile in his voice.

We didn't take small explosions well...and this one could be "Massive," so we cleaned extra well.

Another half an hour later and Nicola walked us inside this cage mid-room.

"Please put these shoes on for grounding and it's alright to hold onto the cage, just don't reach out too far."

"Too far for what," I muttered to the girls?

Ready, steady, "GO!" flipping this large switch on the cage wall started something we, and I do believe I can speak for Olivia and Elsbeth, were not even quite ready for!

Lightening bolts of all sizes, lengths and severity, were shooting at the cage. Yes...the one we were in!

Elsbeth fainted for a moment, to which Nicola was unusually ready as he handed me a bottle saying, "Give her a very mild whiff of what's in it but don't smell it."

It sure straightened her up, with wide eyes too.

We got used to the amazing show for the eyes and sounds of grand crackling we had never heard the likes of.

"This was the foundation for free energy for all the people. It wasn't the time to unleash this on the world as minds had not yet caught up with their own future yet."

"Nicola," I said excitedly, "Now is that time!"

Olivia jumped in saying, "We are hungry for a new energy source.

The glimmer of possibilities spread across his face.

"Perhaps I was just born in the wrong century. Let's see how this one listens."

"You know, my friends, How about a break for a meal or two. It has been some time since my last dinner."

Looking at each other we all laughed, but I'm sure Elsbeth just did, cause we all did, she'll catch up soon.

**END CHAPTER SIXTEEN**

# CHAPTER SEVENTEEN
## I HAVE SOMETHING THAT CAN HELP YOUR FATHER WITH THAT.

There was a loud zap in the basement then a crash. The three of us shot down the banisters...and "So" did Nicola!

In a split of a moment, we were in the basement looking for Dad under a pile of Lord knows what.

As we went to get him up, he winced when we touched his left shoulder. "It's dislocated, I think," Dad said.

"Here, allow me," Nicola asked.

Getting Dad's left arm in what looked like a wrestling hold, told him to take a big breath and then blow out as hard as possible.

In mid blow, Nicola just moved ever so little up, and a pop occurred placing the shoulder back in its socket.

Dad looked up to him saying, "I hardly felt it, thanks so much."

Nicola looked back to us saying he studied all things when he was younger.

We were just happy Dad wasn't hurt worse, as our in house doctor strapped the arm across his chest to heal well.

"I think I'll just draw plans for up and coming work for the next couple of days," Dad said, "But I'm sure you are going to give me the full story on the scientist you have somehow employed at dinner this evening."

"Another plate," Dad asked?

We all shook our heads, but Elsbeth quietly asked, "Will there also be a plate there for me.?"

"Forever," Olivia said.

And she smiled.

Nicola asked if Dad was a good cook, "We all are," I told him. "Tonight, I am almost sure it is Dad's maple candied ham and yam casserole with the little marshmallows on top, with butter milk croissants for dipping."

"Don't know what any of that is, but I'm sure I'm ready," Nicola said with a sparkle of drool on the corner of his mouth.

I think some background classes might be in order, if you don't have any objections," Nicola said.

"Fine with us, we could use some knowledge 'Before' the explosions," I said to everyone's laughs. "Oh, Olivia," I whispered, "Would you grab the last of the cookies and a flask of milk, so we can surprise Nicola with his first twentieth century delight."

Smiling, off she went as the rest of us took up classroom in the kitchen.

## END CHAPTER SEVENTEEN

# CHAPTER EIGHTEEN
## THEY SAY A LITTLE KNOWLEDGE IS DANGEROUS... WE'RE ABOUT TO BECOME DEADLY!

This first class has turned into two weeks of hard study to only grasp the basics of Tesla's genius.

Nicola kept calling Olivia and I the same thing, saying we will be great creators someday. Who knew that "someday" would be now?

Strange as it sounds, his theories were starting to make sense and we both can see them in our minds. Almost as a third dimensional picture laid out in front of our eyes.

From that point foreword, we only asked questions of Nicola, when we may have an idea to improve the current function of a machine.

Amazed, he now went into a higher orbit of mind, asking us, what if, and what would you do?

The import of his work hit the same snag as it did over that half century ago..."Money!"

"Nicola, we have no more extra parts. Worse, we have no money to buy new ones," Olivia said.

"What if we concentrate on one of the more complete lesser ideas and sell one," I asked them both?

He responded, "Fine idea, which one?"

I sat down, handed Olivia a Pepsi and popped one for Nicola.

"Well, we have cell phones with real time, but full sized holograms... that may sell," I said.

Olivia added, "What if we blocked the forward capabilities..."

"Yes, also stop a possible power surge to allow stepping into," I said.

Nicola said, rather loudly, "What are you two up to?"

"The time viewer," we chimed in together.

Nicola was quiet, scratched his head, then said, "Really?"

"Our Uncle Lorenzo works for the National Geographic Society. I'm sure they would be more than excited to get one of these," I said.

Olivia jumped in spitting out, "And every other library in the world!"

Removing the machine to an empty room took three days. We then re-engineered it not to have "future" capabilities. Elsbeth, who has been so patient said, "And so it can't send me back either!"

We all smiled and hugged her saying, "Never."

We invited Uncle Lorenzo over and a week later he arrived, yes, I was named after him, knocking on the front door, Dad answered.

"Lorenzo, what are you doing here?"

"My Niece and Nephew invited me; didn't you know?"

"Apparently not, but welcome to our new, home in the making."

They both laughed and hugged while Dad yelled for us to come down.

"Something you two, well three, wish to tell me?" as Elsbeth smiled.

"Oh, yeah Dad, we created something to sell to Uncle Lorenzo's people," as I secretly winked at him.

"Oh, that, ah, upstairs thing..."

Cutting him off, Olivia said, "Yes," then grabbed Unk's hand while we slid him to the set up room.

As we walked into the door, he stopped, seeing the mirrors, tilted his head as if he recognized them.

Explaining the theory, which wasn't as we had gone far past what we were going to show him, he listened more attentively than usual for an older man to two young teen-agers.

Dad had walked in behind us to see what he was already supposed to have.

"Now don't move without direction, and 'Please' don't touch anything," I asked Dad.

Olivia slowly ramped up the power as I turned the dial.

"One third" and the mirrors began to spin. This brought another head tilt from our uncle and a chin pinch this time.

Then "Two thirds" at which time the sparkle in the center turned into a bright large ball.

The last third was ever so slowly increased to "Maximum" then it happened. A clear picture of a revolutionary battle...

"With sound!"

Well low sound, but able to know what was going on.

Dad smiled, scratched his head, but Uncle Lorenzo fell back against the wall behind him"Do you know what this means?" he shouted!!!

"Well yes," we answered.

"That's why we called you Uncle Lorenzo," Olivia added.

Shutting it down, the memory came to him. "Isn't this a, well visual creation of Nicola Tesla? Although no one ever knew what it did, I do remember seeing this in a large room of his inventions, when I was in school."

"We saw that too and figured how to perfect and build it, did we do wrong?"

"Any patents that may have existed or not, would be long expired today, and anyway, there was never any talk of this in his writings. You kids are geniuses!"

"We only had resources to build this one and no more money to go on." Olivia explained.

Uncle Lorenzo looked at us and then Dad said, "You will never have to worry about money again!"

"If permissible, may I bring two gentlemen over, in two days, for another demonstration? At which point, they will probably wish to hand you a check with more zeroes on it than believable?"

All we could do was shake our heads up and down like crazed people, then hugged him.

Dad had a great suggestion, asking Uncle to stay for dinner.

"Only if you let me take you out for a celebration," Uncle asked?

I felt a tug on my shirt. It was Elsbeth. "Italian food?" she asked. We all laughed agreeing.

As we left for Mr. Romano's Pizza Palace, Uncle Lorenzo quietly asked, "Where might Elsbeth have come from. Her speech and demeanor aren't like that of a twentieth century girl?"

"I looked at Olivia and then at him saying, "You know Uncle, I do believe that someday we shall tell you."

He then said, "But not now?"

We both said, "No....not now."

## END CHAPTER EIGHTEEN
## ANOTHER REALLY LONG ONE ...BUT I WAS HAVING FUN, AND REALLY, ISN'T STORYTELLING JUST THAT!?

# CHAPTER NINETEEN
## THE DAY WAS THERE
## IN AN INSTANT
## WE ALL SHOOK

Nicola started with, "These people coming will be more versed in the ways of electricity. I must teach to you, more than just the basics. But how can I, so much in so little time?"

"I have it, Olivia jumped up saying!" She would learn half and I would learn the other. When one of us got stumped, we'd squeeze the other's hand to take over.

"Genius," Nicola said!

He split us up, Elsbeth coming with me, and Olivia across the room at the other chalk board. We were back to back, so as not to snoop and waste time.

Time flew, and we remembered massive amounts according to our teacher.

Two days of the same and we still were a bit shaky.

"You know, I have an invention somewhere in the house that allows remote talking," Nicola mumbled.

"That's it," said a bit too loudly scaring Elsbeth! "Our ear pod for music." Olivia knew.

With a bit of rewiring, Nicola can hear and speak from another room if we give him the "High" sign.

"Like what?"

"One of us will clear our throat... like "A-hem.""

"That'll do it," Nicola said excitedly.

We decided that now would be a good time to take our places, and then we heard the big round clapper against the front door.

Dad opened it, shook hands with the two well dressed men and hugged his brother, our Uncle Lorenzo, seating them in the kitchen as we had requested, with the smell of chocolate chip cookies baking in the oven. Thanks to Dad.

"Well, sir, we are happy to finally meet you," one of the men said.

"Oh no," Dad said, stopping him.

"The genius ones sit across from you. Now if you want a house built call me. They are the wonder kids as you will come to find out!"

With a bit of confusion, they turned to us, held out their hands and excused themselves for not knowing that from the start.

"My name is Cyrus Smith and He is Morton Jones." "Yes," he laughed, "Smith and Jones!"

Now, may we see this new "Wonder of the World" as your Uncle describes it?"

"This way please," we both said.

Up to the room, separated from all other things, we had set up chairs for them to watch... including a glass of milk and excellent chocolate chip cookies.

I explained my part, then Olivia, hers perfectly. I only hope we do as well with questions.

Olivia wiped any dust from the mirrors as I set the controls.

We had Elsbeth throw the switch on a hand wave, then we started.

Turning to first setting, the mirrors started to turn, giving off a slight sparkle.

The next setting made grand sparkling, then the ball of light started to compress in the center.

The third and final setting that we had left on the machine, flared out, leaving, when our vision cleared, a large panorama of a scene in the 1700's on the east coast of the United states.

There was total silence, then we heard a crash. It was Mr. Jones' milk glass that he dropped.

"Watch and listen," I said giving it the last bit of juice we allowed it.

Mr. Smith said, "Voices, I hear voices!!"

Holding my fingers over my lips he quieted down.

"THEY CAN HEAR US," Mr. Smith squealed?!! Shaking my head whispering "Yes" he became very quiet.

Changing the settings, we went a bit farther back to the early 1600's as even Uncle Lorenzo was "Struck mute" (couldn't talk).

"This concludes the morning special for now," as I turned it off.

They both stood up, started waving their arms and not saying an understandable words.

"See, I told you that you wouldn't have words for it," Uncle Lorenzo said with a large grin.

They sat back down, kept shaking their heads as Elsbeth gently put cookies in their mouths,

which seemed to help.

## END CHAPTER NINETEEN

# CHAPTER TWENTY
## "I HEARD IT ALL!"
## "YOU GUYS DID GREAT!"
## NOW WHEN HE SAYS MONEY,
## JUST SAY HMMM.

Mr. Jones said they were not quite prepared for what the magnitude (Hugeness) of our discovery was and if they may have a few moments alone to discuss.

Down the hall they went, but as excited and almost upset with each other, we could hear most of it.

So, could Nicola, in another room, who by now was chattering about how to respond to their first offer.

"First offer," Olivia squealed a bit loud enough to have the two of them look up to see what "was the matter."

We just waved and smiled, Elsbeth did too.

They came back and spoke to my Dad, asking if he would join in as we were well under age.

He said, "These two are so capable of handling themselves, I would only get in the way, but I will be right here if they need me." They nodded and looked towards us.

Nicola, from the other room, said one word in our ear pieces, "Ready?"

"Yep," I said, and it was on.

Mr. Jones looked to Mr. Smith saying, "We had not imagined this creation could do half what it does...so we would like to buy 40%, where Nicola grunted so loud, they heard him. They immediately said they could investment $125,000,000.00, payable at 40% immediately and the rest over three years

Lorenzo and Olivia would still retain a 60% ownership in the invention.

Tesla was speechless, but I remembered his words, tapped my fingers and said, "Hmmmm."

This seemed to set the two of them on a mental fry down and My Smith blurted out, $150,000,000.00 with "Half up Front! That would be $75,000,000.00 immediately, plus the balance over three years for 25% of the product!"

I said, "Mister, I will be the calm headed one and agree to the last offer." Tesla, we think, was dancing and singing in the other room, as we pulled the ear buds out and secreted them into our pockets so as not to hear him hooting and squealing!

Olivia and I grabbed Dad's hand all shook with Mr. Smith and Jones. Then hugging Uncle Lorenzo, asked if he would like to help run the company.

Shocked, Uncle Lorenzo smiled and nodded.

Mr. Smith asked if, on the way out, he and Mr. Jones might be able to get a few of those superb cookies, as he said a lot of their energy was just expended (Used up) and besides, they loved them?

On the way out, we handed them a bag each with a dozen chocolate chip family specials and off they went.

From the car they yelled that they'd be by right after the banks opened in the morning.

Off they drove, leaving two teenagers, one Dad and an uncle, stealing cookies, all shaking their heads in amazement of what just took place.

## END CHAPTER TWENTY

# CHAPTER TWENTY-ONE
## TIME FOR A FAMILY BUSINESS COME CLEAN MEETING & A PINKIE SWEAR SECRET!

Uncle Lorenzo is our Liaison for Sales.

Dad will simply be called "Our Protector, the most important position of all. We told him, "That means, Dad, that you're our Dad at Work too!" He had the biggest smile on his face.

Then I said, "Now, Uncle Lorenzo, we need a very special 'Pinkie Swear' moment," holding up our little fingers, waiting for him to follow.

In a semi-confused movement, he put it up and we all locked pinkies swearing "Never" to disclose what we were about to show him, our "Secret of Secrets."

He nodded saying, "I promise."

At that point, I put my ear bud back in and turned the microphone back on and asked our friend in the other room to join us.

Still confused, we had Uncle Lorenzo turn around and face our friend who had been waiting in the other room and was now coming through the door.

"This, Uncle Lorenzo," Olivia said, "is an important part of all this...meet Nicola." At which point, my Uncle looked, then visibly spazzed.

"Nicola TESSSLAAA!!!!?"

"Olivia, James," He stammered (jumbled talk). "He, HE's..."

"Yes, we know Uncle Lorenzo," Olivia answered giggling at his facial twitches upon seeing Nicola.

"This is our partner, teacher, and resident genius, Nicola Tesla," I said.

Uncle Lorenzo, shaking all over, attempted to extend his hand to shake our surprise for him, but couldn't quite do it.

Dad took Lorenzo's hand, and took Nicola's hand, completing a three handed shake.

Olivia said... "Why don't we have a little snack and go over all this, Okay?"

Addressing Renzo, Nicola said, "After some more cookies and milk?" "I have so many inventions to go over with you, Olivia and Renzo. Plus, I have an idea for a new propulsion method for airplanes that can make a transcontinental trip in less than an hour.

We all walked down the stairs, with Nicola's arm over Olivia, Uncle's arm over him, followed by Elsbeth. Dad and I were just shaking our heads, and me saying, "This is how I'll remember, it started, always."

## THE GRAND BEGINNING

P.S. Nicola leaned over, whispered to us  as we went downstairs, "Did you ever find my stash of coins and monies from all over?" We shook our heads, "Yes."

"Did you see the bag of pyramid shaped coins?" Again, we shook our heads "Yes," only this time, with a lot more curiosity. Nicola said, "Well, just wait till I show you where "They" came from...and what that tall marble Cupola is in the back!" (Cupola...a dome atop these pillars.)"

Our eyes opened wide now, as he stood back straight up, smiling like a cat with a big bowl of milk and asked out loud, "What's for 'Lunch,' I'm famished, (Look this one up) as he walked with Dad with Uncle Lorenzo, whistling down the hall, Elsbeth close behind them.

I looked at Olivia, and smiled that excited smile, and quick stepped to keep up, not wanting to miss,

The "Next" thing he would tell us!
Now,"That's"... A great Beginning!!

Olivia Eleanor
&
Lorenzo Maximilian
Oh...don't forget Elsbeth & Nicola!


MMXVI...
AND BEFORE!


For Whom the Book Reads...
This tale is for my newest smiley Grand Babies
And My Next to the Oldest
Olivia & Brother James
And Lorenzo
I hope that when they are old enough, they will read it, and say and know it was written just for them.
Be well my Olivia, James & Lorenzo, enjoy wonderful Imaginations.
Love
Grandpa Mike

Elua tausani he umikumamaono
ДВЕ ТЫСЯЧИ ШЕСТНАДЦАТАЯ
ΔΥΟ ΧΙΛΙΑΔΕ Σ ΔΕΚΑΕΞΙ
ԵՐԿՈՒ ՀԱՉԱՐ տասնվեց

The first three who tell me what is the message in any of these languages...and is under 18, send me a message at

mromano5150@gmail.com will receive a free book of your choice from my web page. And maybe...just maybe, I'll put you into one of my next books!!

You can see all of our books there for your choosing and can read the first two chapters of each book if you go Amazon through our web page and click on book to open them.

And with their permission, hers or his name in the next book as the Winner!!

Good luck and great Imagining!


Michael
Your Imagineer

On an odd note... as with many science fiction films, their creations have become reality.

I know it may be pompous to expect, but I do believe some of these machinations from my mind ... will become reality someday.

Hope I'm around to see them
Mike


See you at
Storiesbymikeromano.com

www.ingramcontent.com/pod-product-compliance
Lightning Source LLC
Chambersburg PA
CBHW052054150726
48002CB00002B/883